For my mom, who helped me become the writer I am today.
I forgive you for insisting I wear a sweatshirt with my
Halloween costume in 1983. —L.G.

For Steve, who likes to make
people laugh on Halloween. —J.W.

Farrar Straus Giroux Books for Young Readers
175 Fifth Avenue, New York 10010

Text copyright © 2016 by Laura Gehl
Pictures copyright © 2016 by Joyce Wan
All rights reserved
Color separations by Embassy Graphics
Printed in China by Toppan Leefung Printing Ltd.,
Dongguan City, Guangdong Province
Designed by Anne Diebel
First edition, 2016
1 3 5 7 9 10 8 6 4 2

mackids.com

Library of Congress Cataloging-in-Publication Data
Gehl, Laura.
    Peep and Egg: I'm not trick-or-treating / Laura Gehl ; pictures by Joyce Wan — 1st ed.
        pages   cm
    Summary: "Egg is too scared to go trick-or-treating, until Peep finds a way to help her overcome her
fears"—Provided by publisher.
    ISBN 978-0-374-30122-4 (hardcover)
    [1. Chickens—Fiction.   2. Eggs—Fiction.   3. Sisters—Fiction.   4. Halloween—Fiction.   5. Fear—Fiction.]
1. Wan, Joyce, illustrator.   II. Title   III. Title: I am not trick-or-treating.

PZ7.G2588Pe 2016
[E]—dc23

2015012439

Our books may be purchased in bulk for promotional, educational, or business use.
Please contact your local bookseller or the Macmillan Corporate and Premium Sales Department
at (800) 221-7945 ext. 5442 or by e-mail at MacmillanSpecialMarkets@macmillan.com.

PEEP and EGG

I'm Not Trick-or-Treating

LAURA GEHL

Pictures by JOYCE WAN

Farrar Straus Giroux • New York

"Trick-or-treating is going to be
so much fun," Peep said.

"Are you ready yet?"

"Too scary," said Egg.
"I'm not trick-or-treating."

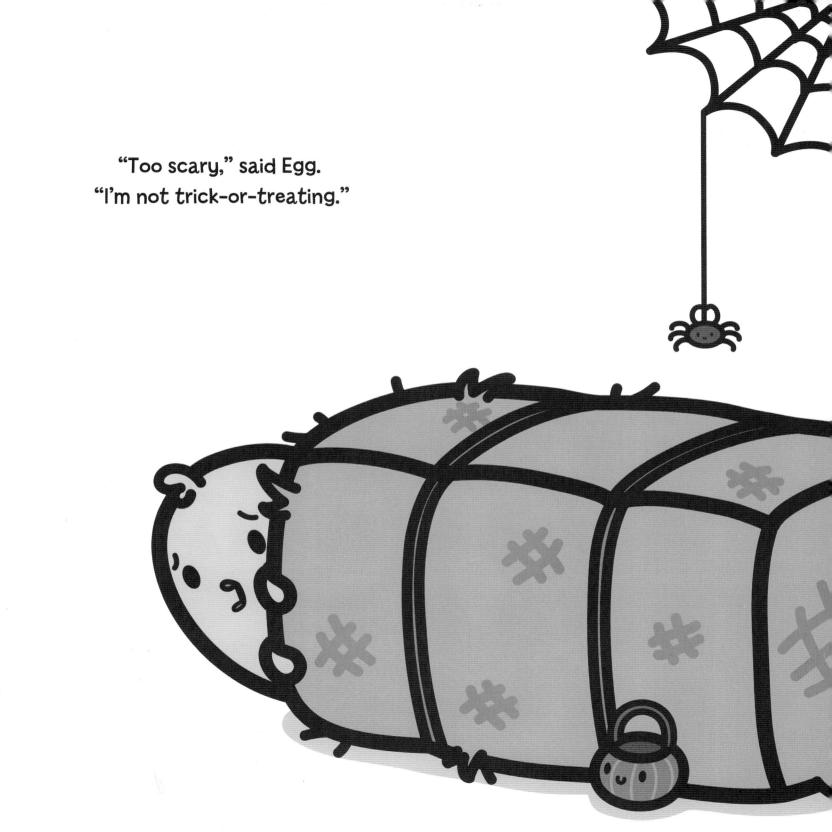

"Let's just put on your costume," Peep said.

"I'm not trick-or-treating," said Egg.

"Our first stop will be down at the duck pond," Peep said.

"Vampires!" said Egg.
"I'm not trick-or-treating."

"Then we'll climb through the fence and visit the cows," Peep said.

"Mummies!" said Egg.

"I'm not trick-or-treating."

"Want to hear a Halloween joke?" Peep asked.
"Laughing might make you feel less scared."

"I'm not laughing," said Egg. "And I'm not trick-or-treating."

"What do you call a witch at the beach?" Peep asked.

"A sand-WITCH!"

"Witches!" said Egg. "I'm not trick-or-treating."

"What fruit do ghosts like to eat?" Peep asked.
"BOO-berries!"

Egg giggled, then shivered.

"Ghosts!" said Egg.

"I'm not trick-or-treating."

"What is a monster's favorite treat?" Peep asked.
"Ice SCREAM!"

"Monsters!" said Egg.

"I'm not trick-or-treating."

"How about if we go to the barn first?" Peep asked.
"Don't you want to see everyone else's costumes?"

"I'M NOT TRICK-OR-TREATING!" said Egg.

"Okay, I'll see ya later," Peep said.
"I'm sure you'll be ready next year."

"Hey! Peep!" called Egg. "Peep! I want to come with you!"

"Peep! Where are you?"

"Peep! I can't find you!"

"Did you have trouble putting on your costume?" Peep asked. "I'll help."

"Here's one last joke," Peep said.
"What do birds say on Halloween?"

"I know," said Egg. "Trick or TWEET!"

"I'm glad we went trick-or-treating," said Egg,
munching happily on a piece of candy.

"Me too," Peep said. "Happy Halloween!"